It's probably one of those big Japanese robots...

Kyle, Jason, and Jenny peered into the box. Looking up at them from inside was a brown, long-eared, furry—"Fat, snaggle-toothed, dumb RABBIT!" Kyle jeered. "Not *robot*!"

"Great prize, Brown!" Kyle laughed loudly and walked away.

"Oh, yeah?" the voice rasped. "You're just jealous, you dumbbell!"

Kyle whirled around. "What did you say?" he asked threateningly.

"Um, er," Jason stammered, "n-nothing." Kyle was a year older than he was, and bigger. Besides, Jason *hadn't* said anything.

"I'll get you later," Kyle muttered as he stalked away.

Jason and Jenny were finally alone, except for the rabbit.

"Who said that stuff?" Jason demanded.

Jenny pointed at the box at their feet. "I think," she said in a small voice, "it was the *rabbit*."

BAD NEWS BUNNY

#1
THIRD-PRIZE SURPRISE
SUSAN SAUNDERS

Illustrated by LARRY ROSS

A MINSTREL BOOK

**PUBLISHED BY
SIMON & SCHUSTER, INC.**

TO ARTEMIS,
who has a bunny herself

This novel is a work of fiction. Names, characters, places and incidents are either the product of the author's imagination or are used fictitiously. Any resemblance to actual events or locales or persons, living or dead, is entirely coincidental.

A MINSTREL PAPERBACK *ORIGINAL*

 A MINSTREL BOOK, published by
Simon & Schuster, Inc., 1230 Avenue
of the Americas, New York, New York 10020

Text copyright © 1987 by Susan Saunders and Cloverdale Press, Inc.
Illustrations and cover copyright © 1987 by Larry Ross

ISBN: 0-671-62713-9

First Minstrel Books printing March, 1987

10 9 8 7 6 5 4 3 2 1

BAD NEWS BUNNY, A MINSTREL BOOK and colophon are trademarks
of Simon & Schuster, Inc.

Printed in the U.S.A.

BAD NEWS BUNNY

#1
THIRD-PRIZE SURPRISE

chapter 1

"Why should I buy a raffle ticket?" Jason Brown asked. "I never win anything."

"That's not true," his little sister, Jenny, argued. "You won a door prize at the Friends of the Park supper."

"Yeah," Jason said flatly. "That was great—a toaster with four slots."

"But this is different," Caroline Clements told him. "The prizes are neat. First prize is a red ten-speed bike!"

Caroline was in Jason's fourth-grade class at Birchwood Elementary. She was also the Browns' next-door neighbor, so they usually walked to school together.

"Don't be so cheap, Jason," Jenny said. "The tickets are only twenty-five cents each, and the money goes to buy new books for the library."

"Hey—wait up!" someone called from behind them. "Hello, Kyle!" Caroline squeaked excitedly. Kyle Johnson was a fifth grader who lived down the street. Caroline had told Jason she thought Kyle was the cutest boy in school.

"That makes two of you who think so," Jason had answered. "You—and Kyle!"

Obviously, Caroline didn't care if Kyle was conceited.

She was gazing at him with a sickening smile on her face.

Kyle flashed her his glossiest grin. "I'll take eight of those raffle tickets," he said to Caroline. He pulled out two crisp one-dollar bills and handed them to her with a flourish. "I hope you haven't bothered to buy any, Jase," he added smugly to Jason. "You don't have a chance to win the bike—I'm feeling too lucky."

"I'll take a ticket," Jason told Caroline, glaring at Kyle.

Kyle just smiled and shrugged his shoulders. He tucked the tickets carefully into his shirt pocket. "You're just throwing your money away," he said over his shoulder.

"Isn't he incredible?" Caroline gushed. Even Jenny was looking pretty impressed. Jason handed Caroline two dimes and a nickle, and she tore off a ticket for him from her book. "Come on!" he snapped. "We're going to be late for school!"

Jason slid into his seat just before the final bell rang. He was still clutching his raffle ticket.

"How many tickets did you buy?" whispered Tommy Selden from the desk next to Jason's.

"One," Jason muttered, stuffing the ticket into the pocket of his pants.

"I bought ten!" Tommy told him. "I had to empty my bank, but it'll be worth it — the first prize is a bike!"

Everybody thought he was going to win the bike! "What are the other prizes?" Jason asked.

"Uh—I think second prize is a radio," Tommy answered. "I can't remember the rest. The list's on Mr. Howard's office door."

Mr. Howard was the Birchwood principal. "Quiet down back there," Miss Wilson, their teacher, warned from the front of the room. "Class, take out your math notebooks."

There was a crowd around Mr. Howard's door at recess. Jason stood on his tiptoes, but he couldn't see over the heads of the other children in front of him.

Tommy was just tall enough, however. "I'll read it to you," he volunteered.

The list was handwritten by Mrs. Hopkins, the librarian, in small, crabbed letters. Tommy was not a great reader—he leaned forward, squeezed up his eyes, and sounded out the words. "Fir-rst prize. Bi-cy-cle from Sam's Bike Shop. Second prize. Ra-dio from RCI. Third prize. R-ro-b-bot from Amy's Empo-or-i-um. Fourth prize. Gift cer-t-ti-fi-..."

"Thanks," Jason said. At least there wasn't a toaster in the bunch.

The raffle was held in the gym when school was over that Wednesday. Mr. Howard stood on the stage in front of a microphone. On one side of him was a large wire cage crammed with ticket stubs. On the other side was the first grader he had chosen to pick the winners. The red ten-speed stood behind him.

First Mr. Howard made a short speech about the store owners who had donated the prizes. Next he talked about how much money had been made for the library through ticket sales: almost seven hundred dollars!

Then the drawing began. Mr. Howard spun the wire cage. The little pieces of paper whirled around and around. He asked Sally, the first grader, to reach in and pull out a stub.

"The winner of the fifth prize, a pocket calculator from Carson's Pharmacy," Mr. Howard announced, "is number five hundred eighty!"

"That's me!" a fifth grader spoke up. He walked to the stage and took the box from Mr. Howard.

"All right," Mr. Howard said, spinning the cage again. "Please pick another one, Sally."

Fourth prize, a twenty-five-dollar gift certificate for records and tapes, went to Marcy Hopkins, a second grader. Then Mr. Howard spun the cage, and Sally drew another stub.

"The third prize, from Amy's Emporium, goes to number six hundred forty-seven!" the principal said.

Six hundred forty-seven!

"Jason!" Tommy Selden said, pounding Jason on

the back. "That's you, Jason! You won the robot!"

"I can't believe it!" Jason mumbled. "I've actually won something good!"

"Congratulations, Jason," said Mr. Howard, handing him a large box. "Don't drop it—it's heavy."

It's probably one of those big Japanese robots, Jason decided.

Jenny left her group of third-grade friends and raced across the gym to look at her brother's prize.

"It's a robot," Jason told her. He set the box down on a bench. "I just want to see who wins the bike."

Second prize—the radio—went to a girl in Jenny's class, Susan Evans.

"And now," Mr. Howard announced, "for the grand prize, from Sam's Bike Shop..." He spun the wire cage around and around. "All right, Sally, go ahead...."

Sally reached in, pulled out a stub, and handed it to Mr. Howard. "The winner of the brand-new, red ten-speed bike is...number two-twenty-six!"

Kyle Johnson was standing at the edge of the stage with his tickets in his hand. Jason saw him check the numbers, then wad the tickets up in disgust.

From the disappointed look on Tommy Selden's

face, Jason knew he hadn't won the bike, either.

There was a noise at the back of the gym. "Two-two-six!" It was Mr. Keeler, one of the school custodians, waving a ticket in the air. "My granddaughter will love this!" he shouted. He wheeled the bike off the stage to a big round of applause.

"Okay," Jason said to his sister. "Let's go— I'll unpack this at home." He leaned over to pick up the box...and he thought he saw it wiggle a little.

"That's funny." Jason noticed a couple of holes had been punched in the side of the box. "Maybe the robot got switched on by accident."

As they walked out a side door of the gym, Jason and Jenny almost bumped into Kyle.

"Guess you weren't as lucky as you thought, huh?" Jason couldn't help saying. "Aren't you going to open it?" Kyle asked, eyeing the box Jason was carrying. "Is something wrong with your prize?"

"It's one of those big Japanese robots, and I don't want to lose any of the pieces," Jason informed him.

"Robot?" Kyle snorted. "That's not what the list said!" Jason wasn't going to argue. He put the box down on the lawn. He peeled the tape away from the top. He pulled back the flaps, one at a time.

Kyle, Jason, and Jenny peered into the box. Look-

8

ing up at them from inside was a brown, long-eared, furry... "Fat, snaggle-toothed, dumb RABBIT!" Kyle jeered. "Not *robot*!"

Tommy Selden had read the list wrong! "Great prize, Brown!" Kyle laughed loudly and walked away.

Jason and Jenny stared down at the rabbit and then at each other. Before either of them could say anything, they heard a tough, gravelly voice.

"Oh, yeah?" the voice rasped. "You're just jealous, you dumbbell!"

Kyle whirled around. "What did you say?" he asked threateningly.

"Um...er..." Jason stammered, "n-nothing." Kyle was a year older than he was, and bigger. Besides, Jason *hadn't* said anything.

"You'd better not have!" Kyle scowled. "Or you'll be really sorry!"

He wasn't out of earshot when the gravelly voice spoke again. "Yeah? Says you and what other five people, you creep?"

"That does it!" Kyle advanced on Jason with his fists clenched.

Just then, Miss Wilson came out of the side door. "Hello, boys," she said. "Hello, Jenny." Miss Wilson looked into the box. "My, what a cute rabbit."

"I'll get you later," Kyle muttered under his breath before he stalked away.

"Bye!" Miss Wilson said cheerily, and she left, too. Jason and Jenny were alone on the elementary school lawn...alone except for the rabbit.

"Who said that stuff?" Jason demanded.

Jenny looked at him wide-eyed. She pointed at the box at their feet. "I think," she said in a small voice, "it was the *rabbit*!"

chapter 2

"Rabbits don't talk!" Jason replied sharply to his sister.

The rabbit's lips slid away from four big yellow teeth in what looked very much like a grin. "My whole family talks," he said.

The rabbit sat up on his back legs and began smoothing down the fur on his ears with his front paws.

"I've never heard of any talking rabbits," Jenny said slowly.

"And what do you think would happen if anyone had?" the rabbit asked her. "We'd all be treated like freaks, clapped into a zoo, or exhibited from coast to coast in cramped cages, with no home to call our own. Who wants that?!"

Jason and Jenny nodded—the rabbit made sense.

"So you'd better keep quiet about this," the rabbit warned them. "If you tell anybody, I'll never talk again. Then they'll think you've made the whole thing up...and that you're very weird. Understand?"

"Yes," Jason said.

"Yes," Jenny echoed.

"All right, let's go," the rabbit ordered.

"Go?" Jason repeated uncertainly. He couldn't get used to the idea that he was having a conversation with a rabbit!

"To your house," said the rabbit impatiently. "It's hot out here. And I'm hungry."

Jason folded the flaps back down on the box to shade the rabbit from the sun. Then he picked up the box very carefully and headed for home.

"Mom wouldn't let us have a dog," Jenny whispered. "How do you think she'll feel about a bossy rabbit?"

Luckily, their mother was out. Mrs. Brown had

left a note on the back door: "Gone to the store for groceries. Back soon. Love, Mom."

Jenny took the key out from under the doormat and unlocked the door. Jason carried the box with the rabbit in it into the kitchen. He set the box down on the floor and raised the flaps again.

The rabbit sat up on his back legs and looked around. "Nice house," he said approvingly.

"Thanks," Jason answered. He went to the refrigerator. "I think we have some lettuce."

"Lettuce?! Yech!" the rabbit said. "I don't approve of *green* food. Do you have any Ring Dings?"

Jason shook his head. "Sorry."

The rabbit hopped out of the box and over to the open refrigerator. "Let's see..." he said. "I'll have a slice of that pie—chocolate, isn't it?"

"Maybe you'd like some water to drink with it," Jenny suggested politely.

"A bowl of 7-Up on ice—two cubes—would be fine," the rabbit told her.

While Jason was cutting the pie, Jenny asked the rabbit, "Do you have a name?"

"All the males in my family have been named Peter," the rabbit answered. "It's from some dumb story. I'm Peter Rabbit the Forty-Third." The rabbit

thought for a moment. "But I liked what the kid was calling me before—Robot. That's a name you can really get your teeth into. Robot."

Jenny set a bowl of 7-Up down on the floor. Jason put the slice of pie next to it. Robot dug in.

As they watched the rabbit eat, Jason said to Jenny, "I have to think of something to tell Kyle."

Robot sat up abruptly. "You're not going to apologize to that creep, are you?" he asked disapprovingly.

"Unless I want to get punched in the nose," Jason answered.

"No way," Robot told him. "I know some wrestling holds that will stop him cold."

Before he could explain what he meant, however, a car rumbled to a stop outside.

"It's Mom!" Jason exclaimed.

He grabbed the plate off the floor and dumped what was left of the pie in the garbage can. Jenny poured the 7-Up into the sink.

"Would you mind getting back in the box?" Jason urged the rabbit. "We'll take him upstairs," he said to his little sister.

"What gives? I wasn't finished eating yet," Robot complained.

"It's our mother—she has some funny ideas about pets," Jason said. "I thought we'd better break this to her gently."

"The right timing could be very important," Jenny added.

Robot smoothed his whiskers with his front paws. "There's nothing to worry about," he assured the children. "I'll simply hypnotize your mother with my charm."

Mrs. Brown opened the back door. "Jason? Jenny!" she called. "Oh—here you are." She walked into the kitchen carrying a big bag of groceries. "How was school today? Aagh! What is that?!" She had caught sight of Robot.

"It's a rabbit," Jason said artlessly.

"I see that it's a rabbit, Jason," Mrs. Brown replied, carefully putting down the groceries, "but what is it doing in our kitchen?"

"Jason won it!" Jenny told her. "Isn't that terrific?" Mrs. Brown didn't answer. She was staring straight at Robot. He had fixed her with an unblinking gaze, and she was peering deep into his dark brown eyes. An odd, faraway expression came over Mrs. Brown's face.

"Mom?" said Jenny.

Jason looked up at his mother, then back down at Robot. What exactly had the rabbit said? "I'll hypnotize your mother with my charm…." *Hypnotize?* Oh, no!

Not wanting to take any chances, Jason dashed between them. "Stop that!" he hissed at Robot.

Mrs. Brown shook her head and blinked a couple of times. "Jason won it?" she repeated, taking up the conversation where it had left off. "Then he'll have to exchange it for something else—you know our rule about pets."

She leaned around Jason to look more closely at the rabbit. "Although I'll admit you may have some trouble getting them to take it back," she went on. "It's not very pretty, is it?"

"He's very smart," Jason said quickly, knowing how sensitive Robot was to remarks about his looks. Jason already had Kyle to worry about—he didn't want the rabbit making his mother angry, too.

"Oh?" Mrs. Brown replied, sounding doubtful. Jason thought fast. "Yes—I've already taught him some tricks. Want to see?" He turned around to face Robot.

The rabbit was frowning at him. "Tricks?" he growled in his raspy voice.

Jenny coughed loudly to cover up the rabbit's voice. "Please!" Jason whispered. Out loud, he said, "Robot—sit up!"

Slowly, slowly, Robot rose onto his back legs.

"Robot—lie down!" said Jason.

Even more slowly, Robot lay down on his side. "Why don't you make up your mind?" he grumbled.

"Isn't he good?" Jenny practically shouted, so that her mother wouldn't hear the rabbit.

"Robot—roll over," Jason ordered.

With a groan—he had a big, fat stomach—Robot pushed himself over on his back, then flopped down on his other side.

"He does seem intelligent," Mrs. Brown admitted.

"It wouldn't be like having a dog," Jason told her. "He doesn't have to be walked. Or a cat—he won't scratch the furniture. He'll be cheap to feed, grass and weeds and leftover salad...."

"Ick!" he heard from behind him.

"What did you say, Jenny?" Mrs. Brown asked.

"I sneezed," Jenny answered. "Excuse me."

"Coughing and sneezing—are you coming down with a cold?" her mother wanted to know.

"So, what about it, Mom?" Jason interrupted, before his mother could change the subject. "Can we keep him? Please say that we can keep him."

"I want to talk it over with your father," Mrs. Brown said.

"We'll just take Robot up to my room until Dad gets home, then," Jason said.

"Wouldn't the garage be better?" Mrs. Brown suggested.

"He's used to being indoors, Mom," Jason told her. Robot hopped neatly into the cardboard box. Jason folded down the flaps and hustled it out of the kitchen before his mother could say anything more.

chapter 3

"The garage!" Robot rumbled. Not even the closed box could muffle his outrage. "Does she have something against rabbits?"

"Mom's just not used to animals," Jenny explained as she and Jason climbed the stairs.

"At least she didn't say no," Jason said to his sister, encouraged. "That means we still have a chance."

Jason carried the box into his bedroom and set it down on the floor. Robot pushed the flaps back with his head and hopped out. He took a quick look around, and his nose was twitching indignantly.

"Where's your television set?" he demanded.

"I don't have one," Jason replied.

"No TV? I can't live without TV!" Robot's ears drooped.

"We watch television in the den downstairs," Jason told him.

"Oh—that's okay," Robot said. "What time is it now?"

"It's almost five o'clock," Jenny answered. "The wrestling finals are on at five," Robot said. "Let's get the set warmed up!"

The rabbit scampered across the room to the door. "We can't," Jenny said apologetically. "Why not?" Robot wanted to know.

"We're only allowed to watch TV after we've finished our homework," Jason told the rabbit.

"Bummer!" Robot groaned. "It's Tiny the Terrible Turkoman against Loose-Lipped Louie—the match of the century!"

The rabbit's ears drooped even farther. "Amy leaves the television on all the time at the Emporium," Robot said. "We all watch: me, Ace the macaw—not too bright, all he can say is 'hello,' 'goodbye,' and 'come back next week,' but he's good company—and Henry the guinea pig. We like the entertainment kind of sports—wrestling, roller derby, that kind of thing." His ears perked up as he remembered.

"We'll do our homework right now," Jenny said, feeling sorry for him.

"Then we can watch whatever you want, as soon as dinner is over," Jason offered.

Jenny ran downstairs to get their books out of their backpacks.

Robot was quiet for a moment after Jenny had left. Then he said, "Listen—I don't think this is going to work out."

"I think it might," Jason replied, misunderstanding him. "My father likes animals a lot more than my mother does."

Robot shook his head. "No. I mean, you kids will be in school all day, there's no TV to watch, and your mom will probably stick me out in the garage the minute you leave the house in the morning. How am I supposed to pass the time? Hopping around a cage, chomping on lettuce, being a bunny? Bo-o-orringg."

"Oh...yeah," Jason said, his heart sinking.

"So, why don't you take me back to Amy's?"

Robot said to Jason. "You can trade me in for something—an aquarium, maybe, or a bunch of gerbils. If you hurry, we can get there in time to see who wins the match."

Robot hopped into the box. "I think it'll be Loose-Lipped Louie—that pile-driver of his is a real killer."

"I don't want any silly fish," Jason interrupted, "or any little rodents, either." Was he going to come this close to having a really amazing pet, and then have the pet turn *him* down?

"I'll think of something," Jason continued stubbornly. "Just give me a second."

Robot's worried about being bored while we're in school, Jason thought. But if he stays in the den with the television on... No, Mom will never go for that. She wants Robot out in the garage.

What if we set the television up on Dad's workbench for Robot to watch during the day? Jason said to himself. Then maybe he won't mind being in the garage until we get home.

Then Jason tried to imagine his mother agreeing to the plan. "A television set for a rabbit?!" he could almost hear her shriek.

Jason shook his head and started over again. Robot

didn't want to be alone while Jason and Jenny were in school, so...why not take Robot to school, too?

"I know!" Jason exclaimed. "The science corner!"

"Huh?" said Robot.

"The science corner!" Jason repeated excitedly. "In Miss Wilson's class, kids can bring in interesting exhibits and put them on the table in the back of the room. Molly Stanton's ant farm was there for a while, and Kenny Caldwell's caterpillars."

"What does that have to do with me?" said Robot.

"Maybe you could be part of the science corner during the week, and come here on the weekends!" Jason replied.

"I'm supposed to share a table with a lot of bugs?" Robot grumped.

"The bugs are all gone now. The ants got out, and Kenny's caterpillars turned into moths weeks ago," Jason told him. "You won't get bored—there are people around all day long."

"Hmmm," Robot said. "Do the kids bring lunches to school?"

"Sure!" Jason answered. He saw the way the rabbit's mind was working. "Twinkies," Jason said. "Potato chips, and Dipsy Doodles—and Ring

Dings! And just think of all those bags of Fritos."

Maybe it wasn't such a bad idea. "But what about TV?" Robot asked shrewdly.

"There's one in the teachers' lounge," Jason replied. "I've seen it—a twenty-one-inch color set with remote control. You could hop down there as soon as everyone's left in the afternoon."

"All right," Robot agreed. "I'll give it a try."

"Great!" said Jason.

There was just one hitch—now Jason would have to phone Miss Wilson and ask her if it was all right. He'd never called a teacher at home before.

"Maybe I'd better wait and talk to her tomorrow," Jason hedged. "I don't want to be too pushy."

"Pushy is best," Robot told him. "I want this settled right now."

The rabbit hopped out of the room and led Jason into the hall to the phone. He thumped his hind foot impatiently while Jason looked up the number: "Wilson, Alice R., three-two-seven, five-one-six-eight."

Jason looked at the phone, then down at Robot. "I feel kind of funny about..." he began.

"Put it on the floor!" Robot ordered. The rabbit nudged the receiver off the hook with his head and

quickly pushed the correct buttons with his nose. Jason could hear the phone ring once, twice...

"Hello?" It was Miss Wilson!

"Hello," Robot rasped into the phone. "Miss Wilson, Jason Brown would like to speak to you."

"Who is this?" said Miss Wilson.

"This is—uh—his uncle," Robot answered. He nodded his head for Jason to pick up the phone.

Jason sat down on the floor and took the receiver in his hand. "Hello?" he said timidly.

"Jason, is something the matter?" Miss Wilson

asked, with a note of puzzlement in her voice.

"Uh, no, Miss Wilson, I was just wondering...." Jason mumbled.

"Jason, don't be such a wimp!" the rabbit hissed. He jumped up onto Jason's lap and spoke into the receiver.

"Miss Wilson," Robot rumbled, "do you remember the rabbit Jason had in the cardboard box today —a very handsome brown rabbit?" he added.

"Why, yes," Miss Wilson answered. "The rabbit he won in the raffle."

"Jason would like to share that rabbit with the class in the science corner," Robot said in his gravelly voice. "You know, teach the other kids about our furry friends."

"Oh, what a good idea," Miss Wilson said. "I've always liked rabbits myself—I had one named Hops when I was a little girl."

"*Hops?!*" Robot made a gagging noise.

Before he could make any rude remarks about the name of Miss Wilson's rabbit, Jason spoke into the phone again.

"It's okay, then?" he asked Miss Wilson. "I'll bring him home on weekends."

"Yes, let's give it a try. We'll see how it works out,"

28

Miss Wilson said. "I'm sure Mr. Keeler can build a cage for us. Why don't you bring the rabbit in tomorrow."

Jason had just hung up the phone when Jenny scooted upstairs. "Jason, Dad is here!" she warned.

"Try to act like a normal rabbit," Jason whispered. "That means *no* talking and *no* funny noises!"

As his father reached the top of the stairs, Jason said, "Hi, Dad! I won a rabbit in the school raffle!"

"So I understand," Mr. Brown replied. "He's a big one, isn't he?" he added, peering down at Robot.

Robot rolled over on his back and did his best to look fetching.

"He seems very nice," Mr. Brown said, scratching the rabbit's fat, furry stomach. "There is a problem, though," he went on. "Your mother would end up having to be responsible for him while you're at school, and she doesn't really feel comfortable around animals."

"He'll only be here on weekends, Dad," Jason spoke up. "Robot will be part of the science corner in my class during the week."

"Well...all right. Then I don't see why you can't keep him," Mr. Brown said with a smile. "Robot—

that's quite an unusual name for a rabbit," said Mr. Brown, continuing to stroke Robot's soft, brown fur.

"He likes it," Jenny replied.

Mr. Brown gave Robot one last pat. "A rabbit should be a nice, easy, uncomplicated pet."

Robot gave the children a big wink.

chapter 4

Jason had his hands full when he spotted Kyle the next morning—he was carrying Robot in the cardboard box.

Kyle didn't see Jason at first. He was reading something on the bulletin board just inside the front door of the school.

Maybe I can sneak past without Kyle noticing, Jason thought to himself.

That might have worked if Caroline Clements hadn't been right behind him. "Hi-i-i, Kyle!" she sang out cheerfully, smiling and waving her hand.

"Hello, Caroline," Kyle answered.

As he turned to face them, his smile faded. "Brown," Kyle said.

"Listen, whoever said that stuff yesterday, I'm sorry," Jason said quickly. "I don't think it's anything to fight about."

"You actually think I'd bother to fight a little fourth grader?" Kyle laughed rudely.

Jason felt someone staring at him. He glanced down at the top of the cardboard box. Robot's brown eyes were glaring at him from between the slightly open flaps.

Jason just knew what the rabbit was thinking: "You apologized to that dumbbell?" Jason pushed the flaps down.

Now Caroline was standing next to Kyle at the bulletin board. "The talent show! Are you going to be in it this year, Kyle?" she cooed.

"First I have to pass the tryouts," Kyle answered, sounding modest, although he didn't look the least bit modest.

"What's your talent going to be?" Caroline asked him.

"I haven't decided yet," Kyle said, implying he

had so many talents that it would be hard to make up his mind. "I think this year I'll play my electric guitar."

"Electric guitar!" Caroline squealed.

"Yeah—I've been playing for about a year now," Kyle said offhandedly. "I'm getting pretty good."

He turned to Jason to ask, "Going to try out again this year with your card tricks?" Kyle nudged Caroline, who giggled.

For the talent show last year, Jason had learned card tricks and flourishes. He practiced them at home until he could do them perfectly. He had gotten such stage fright at the tryouts, however, that even the simplest tricks fell completely to pieces.

The cards that he palmed off the top of the deck popped out of his hands like grasshoppers. When he did the in-the-air ribbon shuffle, he ended up spewing the cards all over the stage and the judges. The audition was a disaster! Just thinking about it made the back of Jason's neck flush a dark red.

Kyle snickered at Jason's embarrassment. "I'm really looking forward to seeing some more of your magic, Jase," he teased. "See you later, Caroline."

Kyle hadn't taken two steps down the hall, however, when a gruff voice rattled out: "I have a new talent this year—it'll put your guitar playing in the shade."

Kyle wheeled around. "What talent is that, Brown?" he asked quietly, looking dangerous.

"You'll just have to wait and see at the tryouts," Jenny said, coming to Jason's rescue.

"I have to go," Jason said, heading for the safety of Miss Wilson's class.

As Jason hurried along, he gave the box an irritated shake. "What did you have to say that for?" he whispered to Robot.

"That little cheesehead gets my back up!" Robot answered.

"But what am I going to do for the tryouts?" Jason said despairingly.

"Can't you play a musical instrument?" Robot asked.

"No," said Jason.

"Sing?" asked Robot.

"No," said Jason.

"Dance?" asked Robot.

"No." Jason shook his head.

"We'll work on something over the weekend," Robot told him. "Don't worry about it." When Jason walked into the classroom, most of the children were already in their seats, waiting for class to start.

Miss Wilson announced from the front of the room, "Here's Jason with the newest addition to our science corner—a nice brown rabbit."

Robot popped up through the flaps on cue. "He sure is big."

"What kind is it?"

"Is it a boy or a girl?"

"Where'd you get him?" Tommy Selden asked. "I won him at the raffle yesterday," Jason answered. "By the way, Tommy, the word on the prize list was *rabbit,* not *robot*."

"Oh," Tommy said, grinning. "Neat."

Miss Wilson had cleared everything off the long table except a large cage made of wood and chicken wire, and several books. "I found Mr. Keeler early this morning," she told Jason. "He put the cage together in no time at all."

"It looks it," Robot murmured.

"Did you say something?" Miss Wilson asked Jason.

"Just clearing my throat," Jason answered quickly. He lifted Robot out of the box none too gently and gave him a little shake before putting him into the cage.

"Notice the way Jason picks the rabbit up, class," Miss Wilson said. "He lifts him by the skin on the back of his neck, with one hand under his hindquarters. Never lift a rabbit by his ears."

Miss Wilson pointed to the books on the table. "Please look through these books when you have a chance. They'll tell you all about rabbits—how many different kinds there are, how they behave, how to handle them, what they eat and drink...."

I'll bet the books don't say a thing about chocolate pie and 7-Up, Jason thought with a grin.

"Tame rabbits eat alfalfa pellets—we have a bag of them right here," Miss Wilson went on, "with celery tops and geranium leaves as a special treat. They must always have fresh water to drink."

"Jason!" Robot hissed, sounding pained.

"I'll take care of the food," Jason whispered back. "Lots of Ring Dings," he promised.

"Now, let's settle down, class," Miss Wilson said. "You can look at the rabbit during lunch. Please take a clean sheet of paper and get ready for the test on fractions."

The rest of the morning went smoothly, although Robot fell asleep and snored loudly through social studies.

At lunchtime, the children crowded around the rabbit's cage.

"Robot is such an ugly name," Nancy Harris said. "He has beautiful soft fur—I think you should call him Fluffy."

Jason said no. "His name is Robot," he told Nancy firmly.

Eric Franco was flipping through one of the books, comparing Robot to the pictures. "I wonder —is he a small Flemish rabbit, a French lop-eared, or a really fat Belgian Hare?" he wanted to know.

Gwendolyn Burke was trying to feed Robot the alfalfa pellets. "He won't eat these," she complained to Jason.

She dropped a few pellets through the wire of Robot's cage. They lay untouched in front of his twitching nose. With a sniff of disdain, the rabbit shifted his position in the cage and turned his broad back on Gwendolyn.

"What do you have in your lunchbox?" Jason asked Gwendolyn.

"Let's see—a peanut butter and jelly sandwich, Fritos, an apple," she answered.

"Try the Fritos," Jason suggested.

The rabbit's ears twitched and he looked up expectantly as Gwendolyn tore open the bag. By the time she had pulled out a Frito, she had his complete attention.

Robot stood up on his hind legs and jerked the Frito out of her fingers before she had poked more than the tiniest yellow corner of it into his cage. A few crunchy bites, and it was gone. Robot scrabbled at the wire with his paws for more.

"He loves them!" Gwendolyn squealed, delighted. Robot was a big success with the whole class. "He's a lot better than the ant farm," even Molly Stanton admitted.

The rabbit was pretty pleased, too. For lunch he had the rest of Gwendolyn's Fritos, half a bag of potato chips, a Twinkie, and two chocolate-chip cookies.

He enjoyed the afternoon classes as well: spelling, music, and French.

With Robot's prompting from the back of the room, Tommy Selden spelled *thorough* correctly. "Thanks, Jason," Tommy whispered.

Jason could hear Robot's gravelly voice joining in as the class sang, "We Are the World." And his French pronunciation wasn't half-bad, either.

"How are you? *Comment allez-vous?*" asked Miss

Wilson. "Now, boys and girls, repeat after me."

"Ko-mon-ta-lay-voo?" Robot repeated along with the rest of the class.

"Very well, thank you," said Miss Wilson. "*Très bien, merci.*"

"Tray biyen, mare-see," rumbled Robot.

"What is your name? *Comment vous appelez-vous?*" asked Miss Wilson.

Robot was getting into the spirit of the lesson. He almost drowned everyone else out with, "Jhuh mah-pell Robot—my name is Robot!"

"Quiet!" Jason hissed over his shoulder.

Jason hung around when school was over for the day. After everyone had left the room, he unlatched the door to Robot's cage. He pushed a chair up to the table. "You can hop onto the chair and then to the floor," Jason told the rabbit. "The teachers' lounge is down the hall to the left."

"Twenty-one-inch color TV with remote control?" Robot said.

"Right," Jason answered. "See you tomorrow."

"Hey, kid!" Robot called after him, hopping out of his cage.

"Yes?" said Jason.

"This is working out just fine," Robot said. He thumped his big back paws on the table for emphasis.

That night, after Jason and Jenny had finished their homework and turned on the TV, Jenny said, "You know, I miss Robot. I wonder what he's doing right now?"

Jason looked at the program schedule. "Ten to one, he's watching *Demolition Derby*," he answered.

Jason knew his rabbit.

chapter 5

So Robot's problems were solved, but Jason's were not. Saturday rolled around, and he was no closer to coming up with a talent for the show.

"The tryouts are Monday afternoon," he pointed out nervously. He was draped across his bed lying on his stomach.

"Take it easy," Robot told him—the rabbit was back in Jason's bedroom for the weekend. "Jenny, put the radio down on the floor, please."

He nudged the dial with his nose until he found a

song with a steady, driving beat. "Let's do some breakin'!" he said to Jason.

"Breakin'?" Jason didn't know what Robot was talking about.

"Break-dancing!" Robot responded.

"I told you—I can't dance," Jason said. "It's not exactly dancing," Robot assured him. "It's more like acrobatics." He turned the radio up loud. "Okay—clap your hands to the beat! One—clap! Two—clap!"

Jason and Jenny both clapped their hands as the rabbit directed.

"Now, bounce your right heel up and down, just to get a feeling for the music," Robot ordered.

Jason managed that all right, too.

"Bend over and put your hands on the floor in front of you," Robot said.

"Then what?" Jason asked.

"Just start walking your feet around clockwise in a circle," Robot told him. "When your feet get close to your left hand, pick it up and put it down behind you, so your feet can continue the circle in front of you."

"Do what?" Jason yelled over the music. "Think of your feet as the hour hand of a clock," Robot explained. "You start with them pointing to six o'clock

and walk them around to about nine. At nine, you pick up your left hand—only your left—and put it down behind you, so that your feet can walk on to twelve."

Jason's feet never made it past nine, however. He collapsed in a tangle of arms and legs.

"Can you do this?" he gasped at Robot. "Of course not," Robot sniffed. "I'm a rabbit. But everybody on *Dance Fever* can."

"Well, I can't!" Jason said grumpily.

He turned off the radio and rubbed a bruised knee. "We'll have to think of something else."

"What about an act Robot can be in?" Jenny suggested.

"Yeah—like a magic act!" Jason said. "Turning raw eggs into doves, and pulling rabbits out of hats!"

"Jason," Jenny whispered so as not to hurt Robot's feelings, "I think it would take a lot more magic to get him *into* the hat than to get him out."

The rabbit's eating habits at school had added an inch or two to his already plump body.

"I see what you mean," Jason murmured. "So I'm right back where I started."

"Maybe Robot could do tricks, the way he did the first day for Mom," Jenny said shyly.

"Absolutely not!" the rabbit thundered. "That was very embarrassing—I felt like a performing poodle!"

"What if you talked?" Jason said. "That would be the best act in the world: Jason and His Talking Rabbit. We'd be famous!"

"Jason," Robot said grimly, "I am not turning myself into a freak for an elementary school talent show."

"What if you talked, only everyone thought it was Jason who was talking?" Jenny asked.

"You mean, like a ventriloquist," Jason said thoughtfully.

Jenny nodded.

46

"The audience would believe I was throwing my voice into Robot, because no one would ever think a rabbit could talk on his own," Jason said.

"Right," said Jenny.

Robot looked suspicous. "What's in it for me?" he wanted to know.

"Wouldn't you like to get even with Kyle?" Jason asked him. "If we had a great act, it would drive Kyle crazy."

"Hmmm," Robot said. "What would we talk about?"

"We could tell jokes!" Jason said, starting to get excited.

"What kind of jokes?" Robot asked, halfway interested. "Rabbit jokes!" Jason and Jenny said at the same time.

"Like, where does a six-hundred-pound rabbit sleep?" Jenny told him.

"Where does he sleep?" asked Robot.

"*Anywhere he wants!*" Jason and Jenny shouted together.

At first Robot sat quietly. Then the children heard an odd, hiccuping sound bubbling out of his throat. He was laughing—Robot was laughing!

"I'll do it," he said when he'd calmed down. He

rubbed an eye with one paw. "On one condition."

"What's that?" asked Jason.

"I get the best lines," replied the rabbit.

"Fine," said Jason.

"You're going to knock 'em dead!" Jenny exclaimed.

chapter 6

By Monday afternoon, Jason and Robot had their act down pat. They had run through the jokes hundreds of times. Robot had even agreed to do a few simple tricks at the beginning of the act, just to ease the audience into it. There was no reason for Jason to be the least bit nervous. As soon as he saw the lighted stage at the end of the gym, however, he felt the old butterflies fluttering in his stomach—stage fright.

Tommy Selden was already there, tossing colored balls into the air—Tommy was a very good juggler.

Caroline Clements had strapped on her red patent-leather tap shoes. She was standing as close to Kyle as she could get, admiring his sparkling blue electric guitar.

Caroline looked up just long enough to point out, "Jason, your face is a really funny color."

"Oh, he'll be okay," Kyle said in a baby voice, "as wong as he's got his wittle wabbit with him."

Kyle was referring to Robot, who was tucked under Jason's right arm.

"Grrr!" Robot growled. He started to wriggle angrily. "Let me at him! I'll give him a couple of rabbit kicks he won't forget in a hurry!"

Jason held on to the rabbit more tightly. He walked to the end of the first row of chairs and flopped down.

The judges were sitting on folded chairs at one side of the stage: Mr. Howard, Mr. Levine, the art teacher, Mrs. Paesano, the music teacher.

"Ulp." Jason mumbled to Robot, "I think I'm going to be sick. Maybe we'd better forget about this."

"Oh no, we won't!" Robot hissed from his place on Jason's lap. "I'm going to make Kyle sorry for every remark he's made about me—*and* you."

Mr. Howard checked his watch. He stood up and

stepped to the front of the stage. "It's four o'clock—time to start the tryouts for the talent show. Who would like to go first?"

"I will," Tommy Selden volunteered.

"Okay. Boys and girls, when you come up onstage, give us your name and tell us what you're going to do, before you start your act. If you have a tape you want played, give it to Lucy here."

Lucy, a third grader, stood next to a large tape deck.

"Go ahead, Tommy." Mr. Howard sat down again. Tommy climbed the stairs at the edge of the stage. "Tommy Selden," he said. "I'm going to juggle."

The judges wrote that down in their notebooks.

Tommy wasn't at all upset by having to perform in front of them. He juggled three colored balls, then five. Next he juggled some metal rings. To finish up, he juggled an apple, an orange, and a small grapefruit. As he said to the judges, "The good thing about my act is, I can eat my props when I'm done."

All three judges clapped loudly when Tommy bowed at the end of his act. They scribbled furiously in their notebooks.

"Where did you learn to do this?" Mr. Levine asked.

"My grandmother taught me," Tommy answered proudly.

"Thank you very much, Tommy," Mr. Howard said. "The names of the people who make the show will be posted on my office door tomorrow morning."

"Thank you," Tommy replied. Munching on the apple, he walked down the steps to sit next to Jason.

"How are you doing?" he asked his friend. Tommy knew all about Jason's stage fright.

Jason shook his head and clutched his throat. Tommy nodded sympathetically.

Caroline went next. "I'm Caroline Clements," she announced. "I do tap." She handed a tape to the third grader and stood poised, her arms outstretched, waiting for the music to start. Soon the opening bars of "Tiptoe Through the Tulips" tinkled across the gym.

Both Jason and Tommy sighed. They had seen Caroline tapdance to "Tiptoe" for three years in a row. *Tap-tap, tappety-tap-tap, tappety-tap-tap.*

Robot wriggled impatiently on Jason's lap. "Thank you, Caroline," Mr. Howard said. Caroline rushed down the stairs to stand next to Kyle again.

Jason and Tommy—and Robot—watched a boy

roller-skate to Stevie Wonder. Jenny and four of her friends jumped rope, double-Dutch. Three fifth-grade girls lip-synched to a Pointer Sisters tape. Another girl twirled a baton. There was a skate-boarder, a clarinetist, a violinist who made Robot's ears quiver, and a trumpet player.

Finally there were only two people left in the gym who hadn't performed—Jason and Kyle. Tommy Selden was gone. His mother had picked him up for an appointment at the dentist. Caroline Clements was still around, however.

"Who wants to go next?" Mr. Howard asked, looking out at the emptying gymnasium.

Kyle was playing silent chords on his unplugged electric guitar. He didn't raise his head to answer.

"Kyle wants to be last," Robot muttered. "He thinks that way he'll make the best impression on the judges. But we're going to be so good, the judges won't pay any attention to him at all!"

By that time, Jason was too panicky to say anything. Why had he thought he could manage any better this year than last, he wondered.

The answer sat in his lap. Robot patted Jason's legs with his front paws. "Tell him we're ready!" he rasped in his gravelly voice.

"I can't!" Jason gasped and could hardly breathe.

"You can, and you will!" Robot ordered. Jason found himself on his feet, climbing the steps like a sleepwalker.

"My name is Jason Brown...."

Jason had said it in such a low voice that Mr. Howard had to tell him to repeat it. "And what is your act?" the principal asked.

"Uh...Jason Brown and His Talking Rabbit," Jason mumbled.

"Ventriloquism?" Mrs. Paesano said in surprise. Jason imagined what she must be thinking: Here is a boy who can hardly speak for himself, and he says he's going to talk for someone else as well?

Jason bobbed his head up and down.

All three of the judges scribbled in their notebooks.

"The chairs!" Robot hissed.

Jason put the rabbit down and dragged two chairs out to the middle of the stage. He collapsed onto one of them and held on tight. This is a nightmare, he thought.

"Sit!" Robot prompted in a loud whisper.

Jason stared out into the dark gym—and saw Caroline Clements and Kyle. They were both laughing so hard, they were holding their sides!

Jason sat up straighter. "Sit!" he said to Robot sternly.

Robot sat up on his hind legs as nicely as he could. "Lie down!" Jason commanded.

Robot did so.

"Roll over!" Jason ordered.

Robot rolled over.

"Get in the chair," Jason said, tapping the chair next to him.

Robot jumped up and sat quietly, watching Jason.

"How are you tonight?" Jason asked the rabbit in a loud voice.

"In the peak of health, thanks," Robot rumbled. There were gasps of amazement from the judges. They actually thought Jason was a ventriloquist, asking questions himself and then answering for Robot. It was working!

Caroline Clements had stopped giggling with Kyle. She was sitting in the front row, staring up at Jason and the rabbit.

Now that they had everyone's attention, they moved quickly on to the jokes.

"Where does a six-hundred-pound rabbit sleep?"

"Anywhere he wants!"

"What's the difference between a rabbit and a flea?"

"A rabbit can have fleas, but a flea can't have rabbits."

"What has four legs and sees just as well from either end?"

"A rabbit with his eyes closed."

"When is a rabbit most like a pony?"

"When he's a little hoarse."

"What is a bunny after it is a year old?"

"Two years old!"

By the time they'd gotten to their last joke, Jason was feeling great. "How much do you have to know to teach a rabbit tricks?" he asked.

"A little more than the rabbit," Robot replied with a wink.

Jason stood and took a bow.

The judges applauded wildly.

"Son," Mr. Levine said seriously, "I think you have a future in show business."

"Excellent," said Mrs. Paesano, "just excellent. The rabbit is adorable, and so smart."

"You must have worked on this for a long time, Jason," Mr. Howard added, perhaps with last year's flop in mind.

Borrowing Kyle's glossiest grin, Jason picked up Robot and left the stage.

Caroline was waiting for him at the bottom of the stairs. "How did you learn that?" she wanted to know. "You don't even move your lips. Did it take a long time? Can you teach me?"

Jason, Robot, and Jenny didn't stay to hear Kyle play his electric guitar. Neither did Caroline—she followed them out of the gym, still asking questions.

chapter 7

After the tryouts, Jason and Robot were stars. The other kids at Birchwood Elementary could hardly wait for the talent show, to see them do their act.

"It's great!" Caroline Clements reported to the class the next morning.

"Will you give us a preview?" Gwendolyn Burke asked Jason.

"Yeah—let's see how you do it!" Eric Franco urged.

"You'll have to wait for the show," Jason answered.

Onstage, he and Robot were far enough away from their audience to make the idea of ventriloquism believable. Up close, someone might decide that Robot was doing his own talking!

The list went up on Mr. Howard's door at noon. All those who had made the talent show were on it. Their names were printed in the order in which they would appear on the program. Tommy Selden was in the show, and the roller-skater, and Jenny and her double-Dutchers, even Caroline—and Kyle Johnson. But who was to appear last on the program?

"Jason and His Talking R-R-Rabbit!" Tommy Selden read. "You've got the best spot in the show!" Tommy shook Jason's hand.

"You deserve it," Caroline told him. "Oh—Kyle," she added.

Kyle Johnson brushed past them without stopping, but Jason saw the ferocious scowl on his face.

I think I'll stay out of his way until after the show, Jason thought. *I wouldn't want him to have to break his rule about punching fourth graders.*

Kyle wasn't interested in starting any fights with Jason, however. It was the *rabbit* who was on Kyle's mind.

The talent show was on a Thursday evening. Kyle

went home as usual when school was over that day. But two hours later, he sneaked back to Birchwood.

As Robot had told Jason, he was going to take a long nap that afternoon. "It's important for me to get my beauty rest, so I will look my best on stage," he had said. He was sound asleep when Kyle crept into Miss Wilson's classroom.

The rabbit opened a sleepy eye when he heard the door of his cage squeak open. "Mmph...huh?" he rumbled softly.

Robot caught only a glimpse of Kyle's face before he found himself smothered in the folds of a blue towel. He couldn't bite with his head covered up, but he could still kick. Robot lashed out with his powerful hind legs for all he was worth!

"That won't do you any good, fatso," he heard Kyle mutter through clenched teeth.

The rabbit bucked and struggled to get away, but Kyle just wrapped the towel more tightly around him.

"We'll see how good Jason is with half his act missing!" Kyle growled.

He raced down the hall with Robot clutched to his chest. Then they were outside—Robot could hear the birds singing.

They hadn't gone far when Kyle stopped running. The rabbit heard a door open. Kyle dropped Robot and the towel with a thump.

"Too bad for you that you can't really talk," Kyle chortled. "You could call for help. Dumb bunny!"

The door closed, and a latch clicked shut.

Robot twisted and wriggled and pushed until he had freed himself from the towel. Then he looked quickly around. He was in the school tool shed. There were no windows—and the door was locked from the outside!

Robot was so angry that he just stamped the gravel floor with his back feet for a few seconds. "That creep!" he sputtered. "Kyle couldn't stand to be outdone at the talent show, so he had to resort to rabbit-napping. I'll get him for this!"

The best way to get Kyle would be to make it back in time for the talent show. But how was Robot going to manage it?

First the rabbit tried thumping on the wooden walls of the shed with his big back feet. It didn't make enough noise—no one came to investigate.

He *could* shout for help...but if he did that, he would reveal himself as a talking rabbit, and he didn't want to do that.

"Jason's probably looking for me right now," Robot muttered. "Poor kid. Just when I was curing him of his stage fright, too."

There was no way around it. Robot was going to have to do what any normal rabbit would do: *dig* his way out. He sent the first pawful of gravel flying. "This could take quite a while," he grumbled.

Jason was looking for Robot. When he and Jenny had arrived at Miss Wilson's room to pick up the rabbit, they found the door of the cage standing open. The cage was empty, and the rabbit was gone.

"Where is he? He knew we were coming for him early," Jason complained to his sister.

"Maybe he's watching television," Jenny suggested.

The set in the teachers' lounge was dark. "Robot, Robot!" the children called.

They searched the building from top to bottom, with no luck. The fat brown rabbit had disappeared.

"I can't believe it." Jason exclaimed. "He's run out on me!"

"Let's go to the gym," Jenny said. "Robot's probably already there."

A long line of people filed through the front doors of the lighted gymnasium. Jason and Jenny hurried to the side door and climbed the stairs leading backstage. Caroline Clements was wearing a red, white, and blue costume with spangles. "Hi, Jason," she called out over the click of her tap shoes. "Hi, Jenny —cute outfit!"

Jenny was dressed in a lime-green shirt and shorts, to match the four other double-Dutchers.

Tommy Selden stood in a corner and juggled a tomato, a big yellow onion, and an eggplant. "Mom's making spaghetti sauce tomorrow," he explained. Tommy took a closer look at Jason. "Are you okay?"

"You haven't seen a brown rabbit anywhere around, have you?" Jason asked his friend in a low voice.

"Oh, no!" said Tommy. "Is Robot missing?"

Jason nodded, peering behind a stack of folding chairs, then pushing aside some large boxes.

"Lose something, Brown?" Kyle Johnson drawled, stroking his guitar.

"Uh—no," Jason mumbled. Jenny peeked around the heavy gold curtain that stretched across the stage. "Wow, half the town must be here."

"Half the town," Jason muttered. "Half the town will see me mess up. Robot how could you do this to me?"

Jason's stomach was in a knot, his palms were sweaty, his throat felt so thick he couldn't swallow.

"Everybody ready back here?" It was Mr. Howard. "I'm about to introduce the first performer."

"That does it," Jason groaned. "I'm sunk!"

When Robot finally popped out on the other side of the shed wall, he was dirty, bruised, and tired. "It's a good thing the school is right across the street," he murmured. "I'd better get moving!"

Applause burst out of the auditorium as the rabbit

scampered across the Birchwood lawn. Then a couple of chords were struck on a guitar—loud, electrified chords!

"It's Kyle!" Robot growled, hopping even faster. "He thinks he's going to wind up the show—we'll just see about that!"

The brown rabbit bounded through the door of the gym and straight up the middle aisle. The audience started to titter.

"Look it's a rabbit!"

"Isn't it cute?"

"Where is he going so fast?"

Robot was going straight up the steps to the stage. Now no one was paying a bit of attention to Kyle's electric guitar solo!

Kyle stopped playing. "If Jason Brown would get his dumb rabbit out of here..." he snarled through clenched teeth.

Jason stepped onto the stage—Robot had come back! Before he could pick up the rabbit, however, Robot zigzagged behind the curtain.

As Kyle strummed a couple of high notes, the rabbit kicked his extension cord out of the wall. The music died.

"That'll teach him to mess with the Robot!" the

rabbit rumbled to Jason. "Let's go, kid. We're on!"

"It's Jason Brown and His Talking Rabbit!" Mr. Howard announced hastily.

Robot outdid himself. He sat up, he lay down, he rolled over. He performed his tricks like a gymnast. He even turned a flip in the air, his ears twirling like pinwheels. The audience clapped loudly.

Jason waited until things had quieted down a little to do the first joke.

"Where does a six-hundred-pound rabbit sleep?" Jason asked then.

When Robot answered the riddle in his deep gravelly voice, the crowd was absolutely quiet for a moment. Then they all began talking at once.

"That Jason is great!" "What a talent!" "How does he do it?" "He doesn't move his lips at all!"

Jason's parents were as surprised as everyone else. He could see them sitting in the second row. They looked at each other, then stared up at Jason. They couldn't believe it—their son, a ventriloquist?!

With each joke, the roar of the crowd grew louder. By the time Jason and Robot had reached the end of their act, they had to shout to be heard over the applause. Almost everyone in the audience was standing up and clapping. Caroline, Tommy, Jenny and the double-Dutchers were cheering from the wings. Jason's parents beamed with pride.

Jason picked up Robot to take a bow.

"Thanks for everything," he whispered in the rabbit's long brown ear.

"Don't mention it, Jase," Robot rumbled back. "You and me, we're a team now!"

In the next book, Robot decides not to be left behind when Jason and his Cub Scout troop go on an overnight hike. Find out what lies in store for the obnoxious bunny and his pet human when they find themselves lost and alone in the deep, dark forest in BAD NEWS BUNNY #2: *Back to Nature.*

ABOUT THE AUTHOR

SUSAN SAUNDERS was born in San Antonio, Texas. After earning a B.A. from Barnard College in New York City, she began a career in publishing. She worked as an editor, writer, and designer for several major audio/visual companies and publishing houses.

Four years ago, Ms. Saunders left her position as editor to write full-time. She is the author of over thirty children's books, of which two were Junior Literary Guild selections, one a Book-of-the-Month Club Dragon Magic selection, and one a Notable Children's Trade Book chosen by the National Council for the Social Studies/Children's Book Council Joint Committee.

ABOUT THE ILLUSTRATOR

LARRY ROSS grew up in Philipsburg, Pennsylvania, and now lives in Madison, New Jersey. He has always been interested in art and was an art director in an advertising agency before becoming a full-time illustrator of books and magazines. He is married and the father of two boys, ages ten and twelve, who eagerly read all his books.